JE   Mayer, Gina.
MAY   Just a baseball game

JUST A BASEBALL GAME

BY GINA AND MERCER MAYER

For our Little Leaguer, Zeb,
with love

A GOLDEN BOOK • NEW YORK

Just a Baseball Game book, characters, text, and images © 2003 Gina and Mercer Mayer. LITTLE CRITTER, MERCER MAYER'S LITTLE CRITTER, and MERCER MAYER'S LITTLE CRITTER and Logo are registered trademarks of Orchard House Licensing Company. All rights reserved under International and Pan-American Copyright Conventions. Published in the United States by Golden Books, an imprint of Random House Children's Books, a division of Random House, Inc., New York, and simultaneously in Canada by Random House of Canada Limited, Toronto. Golden Books, A Golden Book, and the G colophon are registered trademarks of Random House, Inc. Library of Congress Control Number: 2002092690
ISBN 0-307-10451-6
www.goldenbooks.com
Printed in the United States of America
10 9 8 7 6 5 4 3 2 1

It was time for baseball to start.
Boy, was I ready!

I had a brand-new glove and a brand-new bat. I went to the park for our first practice. Everybody was there.

My team was called the Critterville
Critters. What did you expect?
This year we had a new coach.

First we had to run around the ball field.

Then we played catch. Some kids got
really upset when they dropped the ball.

I was really good at batting
practice. I didn't even have
to use the tee.

We had a pretend game.
I hit a home run.

I caught a fly ball.

My next turn
I struck out.

Then I missed
a fly ball.

Practice was over and the coach passed
out our uniforms. Awesome!
We all went home. Boy, was I tired.

In a few weeks, it was time for our
first game. I was excited!

I put on my uniform. So cool!

I had breakfast and didn't even
spill very much on my uniform.

Dad took me to the park. My team was there and so was the other team.
They were called the Dinosaurs.

Boy, were they big! I asked Dad if
they were really in the right league.
He said, "Yep."

We were up to bat first. I hit the ball . . .

. . . but was tagged out at second base.

Everybody else struck out.
Then it was the Dinosaurs' turn to bat.
They could sure hit the ball.
We played hard for hours.

Suddenly the game was over.

Oh, no! The Dinosaurs had won 7 to 2! I was all upset until our coach pulled us into a huddle.

He said, "It doesn't matter who wins the game. What matters is that you played your best and had fun." You know, he's right!

I did have fun, and I can't
wait for the next game.